For Isabella.
With special thanks to the original cheeky monkeys,
Sue, Pam and Val.

Help! copyright © Frances Lincoln Limited 2004
Text and illustrations copyright © Christopher Inns 2004

The right of Christopher Inns to be identified as the Author and Illustrator
of this work has been asserted by him in accordance
with the Copyright, Designs and Patents Act, 1988.

First published in Great Britain in 2004 by
Frances Lincoln Children's Books, 4 Torriano Mews,
Torriano Avenue, London NW5 2RZ

British Library Cataloguing in Publication Data available on request

ISBN 1-84507-004-6

Printed in China

1 3 5 7 9 8 6 4 2

HELP!

Christopher Inns

FRANCES LINCOLN CHILDREN'S BOOKS

Doctor Hopper is on emergency duty.
If there is a call on her radio
she will leap into action.

Nurse Rex Barker is helping too.
He makes sure that everything
is ready in case they need it.

All of a sudden
the radio
crackles into life.

HELP!

Doctor Hopper and Rex Barker jump into their ambulance.

The first call is from Smelliphant.
She has sniffed too hard and sucked
something up her trunk.

Doctor Hopper has just the thing
in her special tin.

The pepper tickles
Smelliphant's nose and...

Rex makes a safe catch and
hands Smelliphant her baby.
But there is no time to rest.

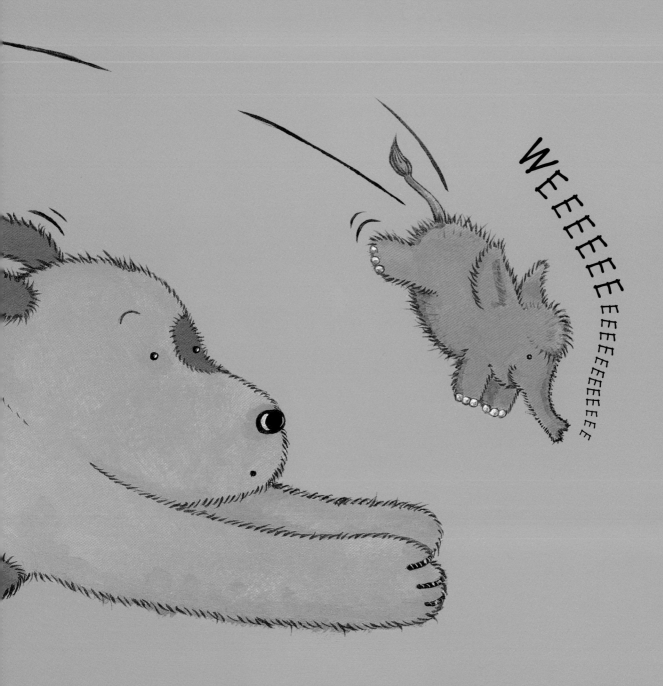

WEEEEEEEEEEEEEEEEEEEEE

There is
another call
on the radio.

DOCTOR HOPPER,
HELP!

Shorty the Giraffe has tied her legs
in knots trying to walk
in her new party shoes.

Doctor Hopper asks Rex Barker
to get the Book of Knots.

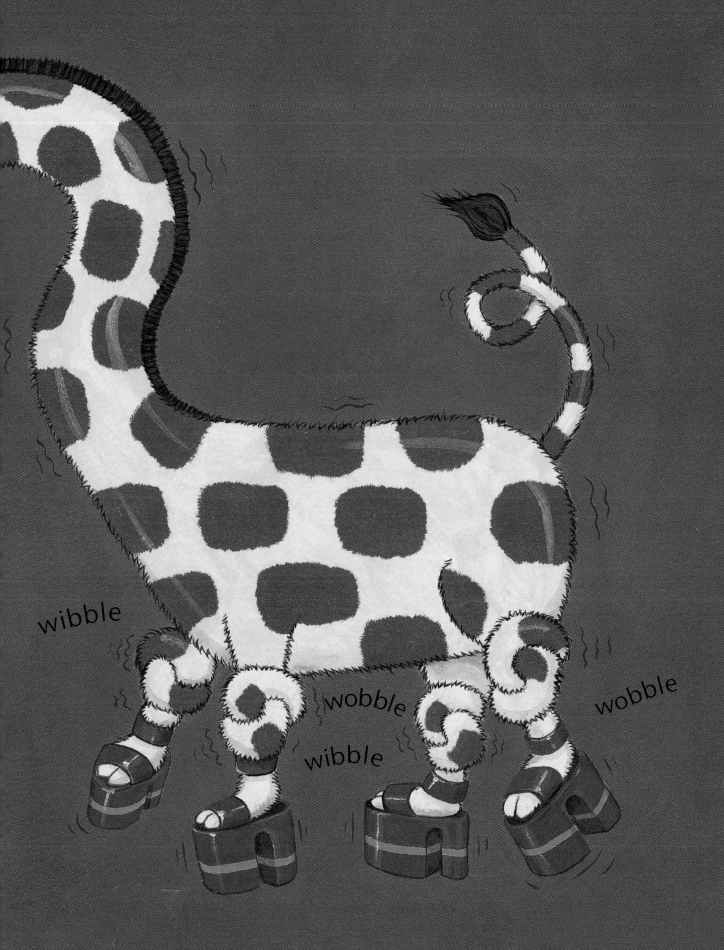

wibble

wobble

wibble

wobble

But Doctor Hopper has forgotten
to put her glasses back on.

Soon Shorty is better...
but the doctor isn't!

Luckily Rex is good at knots too.

Thanks Doc! Thanks Rex!

Once again there is a call on the radio.

Coo-ee, Doctor. HELP!

Pyjama-Case Pig needs help
with her babies. Doctor Hopper listens
to her tummy and decides that it's
time for the babies to be born.

Soon three little pigs are
handed to Rex to cuddle.

But Doctor Hopper knows
there is still another baby to come.

Just one more,
Mrs P.

That's easy for
you to say!

Just then there is a strange sounding call on the radio.

HEELLPP!!!

It is Mr Atomic.
His battery has worn out.

Rex undoes Mr Atomic's back
and Doctor Hopper puts
in a new battery.

But something isn't quite right with Mr Atomic. Doctor Hopper has put the battery in backwards.

Rex turns the battery
the right way round.
This time it works!

The radio
crackles into
life again.

This time it is the Cheeky Monkeys.
But there is NO emergency.
Doctor Hopper and Rex Barker
are not very pleased.

Doctor Hopper tells them off
for wasting her time.

There could
have been someone
who really needed
my help!

The Cheeky Monkeys are very sorry.
Rex thinks of a way they can
put things right.

It's time you
three learnt
to HELP!

So after work Rex shows
the Cheeky Monkeys how
to be doctors and nurses.

This time it's Doctor Hopper
who needs some...

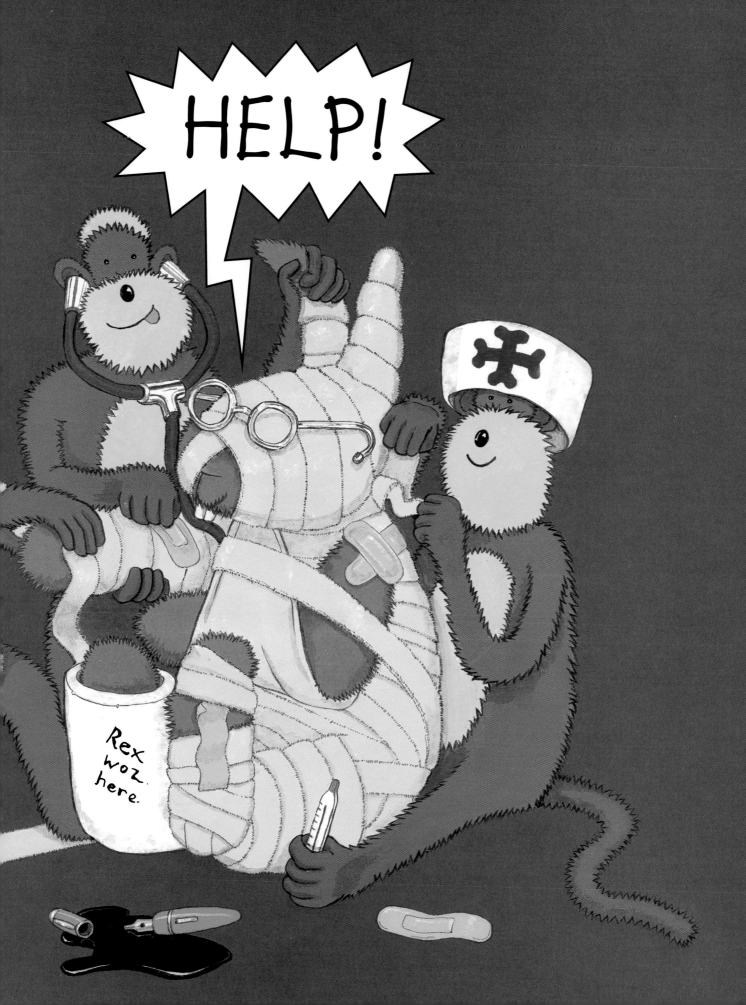